Pal the Pony

Pal Saves the Day

by R. A. Herman
illustrated by Betina Ogden

SCHOLASTIC INC.
New York Toronto London Auckland Sydney
Mexico City New Delhi Hong Kong Buenos Aires

To all the readers who loved Pal the Pony
— R.A.H.

For Paris
— B.O.

ISBN 0-439-57746-2

Text copyright © 2004 by R. A. Herman.
Illustrations copyright © 2004 by Betina Ogden.
All rights reserved. Published by Scholastic Inc.
SCHOLASTIC and associated logos are trademarks and/or
registered trademarks of Scholastic Inc.

12 11 10 9 8 7 6 5 4 3 2 1   4 5 6 7 8 9/0

Printed in the U.S.A.
First printing, January 2004

Pal is the littlest horse on Star Ranch.

He is too little to help the cowboys.

He is too little to round up the horses.

He is too little to herd the cattle.

He is too little to pull the wagon.

Pal is too little to help on the ranch.
So Pal just nibbles some grass
and swishes his tail.

Nibble, nibble. Swish, swish.

But Pal wants to help.
He wants to work like the other horses.

And today is the big square dance
and hayride under the stars.

Most of all, Pal wants to pull
the wagon for the hayride.

But this is Samson's job.
Samson is the strongest horse on the ranch.

Pal cannot pull the big hay wagon.

The sun sets, and all the people arrive.

They all dance and dance
to the music.

The stars start to shine.
It is time for the hayride.

Samson is hitched up
and ready for the hayride.

But Samson is limping.

The cowboys check his hoof.
His horseshoe has fallen off.

Samson cannot pull the hay wagon.

Who will pull the wagon for the hayride?

Kate has an idea.
"Come on, Billy," she says.

Kate and Billy
run to the barn with Pal.

They fill a little wagon with hay.

They hitch Pal to the wagon.

Pal pulls the little hay wagon.

All the children take turns
riding under the stars.

Kate and Billy play music and sing.

It is the best hayride ever.

Everyone calls out,
"Hooray for Pal! Hooray for Pal!"

Kate and Billy pat Pal and say,
"Pal, you saved the day!"